# A ROSE BY ANY OTHER NAME

*Miranda Sapphire*

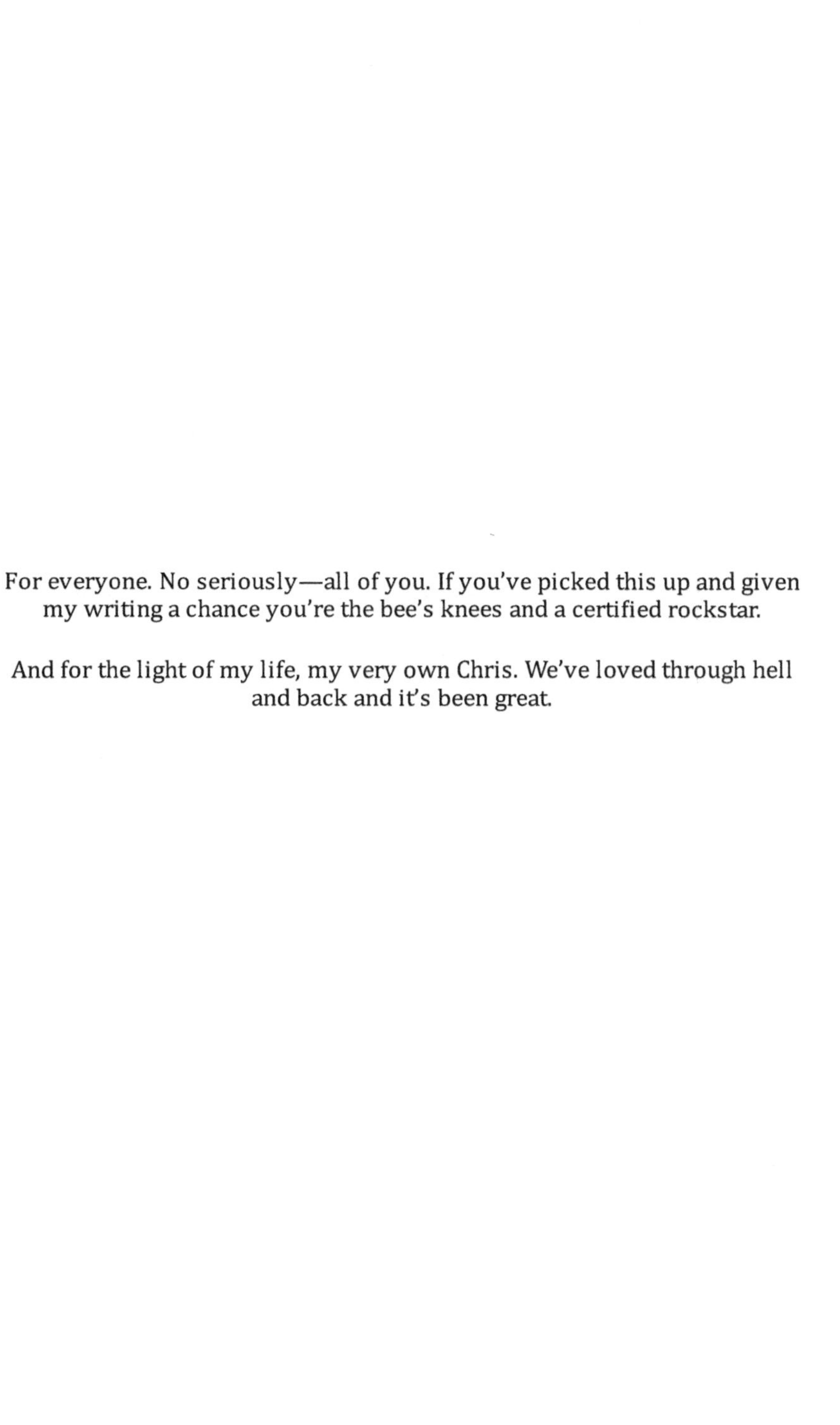

For everyone. No seriously—all of you. If you've picked this up and given
my writing a chance you're the bee's knees and a certified rockstar.

And for the light of my life, my very own Chris. We've loved through hell
and back and it's been great.

# 1



One minute I was kissing my husband Chris goodbye, smacking his sinfully plump ass with all the vigor that beautiful dump truck deserved, and the next I was getting woken up by a knock at my door in the middle of the night.

No body, the officer had said. But the car was totaled, wrapped around a tree out by the freeway, and there had been a lot of blood. Did I have someone I could call? Someone who could stay with me?

Chris. My Chris. The light of my life, my best friend, my tether in the dark. Just…gone. Like he hadn't been a force larger than life, like he hadn't reshaped me into the best version of myself I could ever have hoped to be with his kind smiles and gentle hands.

Just…gone.

I called my sister Sadie, of course. I don't remember doing it, don't remember what I could have possibly said, but I remember waking up the next morning to her blasting her early 2000's pop-punk in my kitchen, making me breakfast.

We both helped with the search when enough time had passed and they still hadn't found anything. I was panicked and desperate, my fingers and toes numb almost immediately in the autumn chill, screaming his name into the wind until my voice stopped working. But I still tried to say it, still kept my feet plodding forward over the crunching leaf fall, stumbling into trees and walking through bushes until my limbs felt like just one big bruise. Chris wouldn't have liked that; he'd have made me turn back and relax in the car, would have grabbed me by my shoulders with his big warm hands and pressed a tender kiss to my forehead as he promised he'd take care of it.

But Chris wasn't here. It almost felt like he was, my heart was crying out for him so loudly. But no matter how many hours I stumbled around in the forest he'd crashed in, we never found him.

After enough time, they told me he was likely dead. I overheard them telling Sadie that an animal must have come along and gotten to his remains before we swooped in with our searches. But that didn't ring true to me. Shouldn't we have found *something*? Even a toe, a scrap of his clothes, some hair—*something*.

Plus…it just didn't feel right. Chris was the center of my universe, so if he was really gone, shouldn't I be feeling it? Shouldn't I be aching with the black hole of his absence? But instead I just felt lonely, and unbalanced, because my other half was somewhere far away from me, but I didn't feel different at the core of me. Didn't feel like I was half dead.

Because of course I'd die without him. I'd known it all along. As soon as he'd pulled me close on that rainy night ten years ago and stared down at me with those molten brown eyes of his, his curly dark hair fluttering boyishly in the wind as we'd huddled in the hut of our bus stop and he'd told me he'd loved me—I knew. There was no way I'd be able to live without that man. So he couldn't be dead, because I was still here.

So I waited. I went through the motions, let Sadie help me with the groceries and the cooking and the cleaning while I did as I was told and declared him dead. We had a service, I pretended to say my goodbyes, and soon enough everyone else was moving on. His mother stopped calling me and inviting me to get-togethers. Sadie went back to her husband, checking in once a week: 9 PM on Fridays like clockwork. My coworkers stopped peering at me all day with pitying sadness, waiting for me to lose it and break down at my computer. So I stopped pretending to be in mourning.

I still wore my rings, obviously. Why would I take them off, when Chris wasn't really gone? I still felt him sometimes, could have sworn I still smelled him all over the house and on the air when I went out for my evening walks. He'd be so mad I was doing them all alone, with how I blasted my music on my headphones and daydreamed; I needed to be more careful, he'd always tell me as he held my hand and followed my meandering paths through our neighborhood. But no one bothered me, because maybe they could sense that he was still with me, too.

3

# 2

With Chris gone, I felt more vulnerable in a lot of different ways, but one of the big ones was that guys were starting to sniff after me again. Even though I still wore my rings and didn't go out on dates, all of my small town's "eligible" bachelors had heard I was a widow and were making their interest known. And without Chris as an excuse I didn't know how to gracefully turn them down.

"Hey Anna, got any plans for the weekend?" my coworker Andy asked me, leaning against the edge of my cubicle and giving me what he'd probably thought was a winning smile.

"Yeah, I'm going to see my sister," I told him, trying to keep my smile bright and my posture relaxed. If I said I wasn't doing anything he'd probably try to ask me out, and since we were coworkers it felt like an even worse idea than seeing anyone else. Chris was the only man I wanted, and I wouldn't settle for Andy, even if he was nice.

"Oh. Well, that's nice. Anything special you're getting up to?"

God, why did everyone have to pry? After the accident everyone had been trying to get the scoop on what had happened, what the updates were, and now that Chris had been declared dead they circled me like vultures trying to find out what I was doing with my free time. Was it morbid curiosity about my being a widow? It was hard to feel like people were just concerned about me when none of them bothered to try and do anything to help me.

I continued to dodge Andy's good-natured interrogation, slipping away when five o'clock hit to finally head home. It had been a long week—all of them were, since Chris had gone—and I just wanted to go home and wait for Sadie's weekly check-in in peace.

It had been almost a year since Chris had walked out the door to pick up some groceries and never come back, our car found wrecked in the forest and covered in blood—Chris' blood. People were expecting me to have moved on by now, the thrill of watching someone else go through the worst thing of their life long since worn off. I pretended that I was fine, that I wasn't in mourning any more, but the truth was that I'd never really gone through it in the first place. I was stuck, feeling like I was just waiting for him to come home, desperate to see him again, to feel his familiar warmth wrapped around me. I still smelled him all over our house, thought I could hear him when I was on the cusp of sleep, telling me how much he missed me, how much he loved me.

I'd never shut off his phone. They hadn't found that, either, had assumed it was with his body. So every night I sent him a text, sometimes called the number and left a voicemail, hoping that I could somehow pull him back to me if I cried out into the void loud enough.

Andy was nice, but he wasn't Chris, and I would accept no less than my husband. I'd told him all the time that he'd ruined me for other men, with his sweetness and his thoughtfulness, and whenever I next saw him I'd be able to shove his face in how right I'd been.

Eventually Andy drifted away, promising to see me on Monday and telling me to have a good weekend, and then I was finally able to slink home.

I drove in a haze, my mind swirling with bittersweet memories of my missing husband. I had a playlist that I put on during my commute, of songs that led me through my most frequent fantasy: walking in the door, downtrodden and wrung out from another long week in operations, only to notice the light on in the bedroom. I would close the front door, being quiet as I could, nervous about burglars and clutching the switchblade I kept in my purse tightly. I'd creep towards the bedroom, heart hammering in my chest, my thumb hovering over the call button on my phone, 9-1-1 already typed into the keypad. The door would be open a crack, and as I'd get closer I'd hear the sound of someone humming a goofy pop song, and then I'd burst into the room, my breath knocked out of me. And there he'd be, covered in dirt and scratches but whole, alive, beaming at me with that beautiful dimpled smile that made me ache, humming whatever song was stuck in his head so he could get it stuck in mine, too. I'd throw down my knife and my phone, and launch myself at him. I'd fling myself into his arms, kissing him with everything I had, crying with relief and tearing at his clothes, at my clothes, so I could feel his skin back against mine at last.

It seemed like I blinked, and then I was home, the sweet haze of my daydreaming still clinging. I threw the car in park and heaved myself out, snatching my purse from the passenger seat and locking it all up. I was so wrapped up in my fantasy that I could smell him, his scent whispering to me on the breeze. I closed my eyes for a moment, breathing deep, trying to catch it, but it was already gone.

I sighed, scrubbing my hand down my face. I was losing it. I was losing my mind, and I didn't care, because if I couldn't have Chris back then I didn't want to be here either. If my body insisted on clinging to life then the least I could do was go crazy.

I trudged up the walkway to my front door, pulling my scarf tighter around my neck against the early autumn chill. I'd lost a lot of weight since the accident, and it seemed like I was always cold now. My friends were all thrilled for me, telling me I looked great, but Chris would hate it. He liked my curves, liked how plush I'd been. My jiggly thighs and soft tummy had driven him wild. Shivering, I dug my keys out and let myself in.

I went inside, absently kicking the door closed behind me, but a quiet grunt stopped me dead in my tracks. I spun around, eyes flying wide, my hand already digging in my purse for my blade.

At first, it was too dark to see who it was—all I could discern in the dim light of the street lights filtering through was the silhouette of a man, filling my doorway.

"C-Chris?" I asked in a whisper, trembling. I knew it wasn't him though; this guy was too tall, the hair too short and straight. I fumbled for the light switch, my cold fingers still digging for my damn switchblade.

I finally found the light switch and flicked it on, illuminating the entryway, letting me see who it was who was following me into my home.

Andy. Goddamn fucking Andy.

"W-what are you doing here, Andy?" I asked, my fingers finally finding my blade and holding it in a tight fist I kept in my purse for the time being. "D-did you *follow me home?*"

He grinned sheepishly, pushing further inside and closing the door behind him. My sweaty palms caused the handle of the switchblade to slide in my grip. "Yeah, I did. Hey, Anna. Nice place you've got, here."

It felt like my brain was going to start leaking out of my ears. Was I missing something? Why was this man standing so casually in my entryway, like he was supposed to be here? "You need to leave, Andy," I told him, keeping my voice low and neutral. "You're not supposed to be here." I felt like I needed to say that for myself as much as I was saying it for his benefit.

He shook his head, holding his hands out in supplication. "Aw, come on, Anna. Don't be like that. We've been dancing around this for weeks. I'm sick of waiting, babe."

Fury spiked, chasing away some of my fear. "I'm not your babe," I ground out, "and I have no fucking clue what you're talking about."

Irritation flashed across his bland face. "What do you mean you don't know? All of the flirting, the talking we've been doing. I know you want me."

I was already shaking my head, trying to ease myself back and away from him. "No, there hasn't been any flirting, Andy. I-I'm still in mourning. For my husband. I'm not—"

"Listen you little bitch," he snarled, surging forward to clamp his hands around my upper arms, wrenching my fist from my bag. Luckily he didn't notice the handle of the switchblade. "I've come all the way over here, and I've been a real nice guy about all this, but you are *not* going to get cold feet on me. I won't let you."

He dragged me even closer, the stink of old coffee thick on his breath, and he lowered his head, clearly meaning to kiss me. I tried to yank myself free, throwing all my weight backwards, trying to get away without having to use the blade. I'd never had to use it before, and the idea of having to slice through flesh, to use it to hurt or kill another living person, was hitting me harder than I'd thought it would.

I almost brought him down on top of me, but my ploy worked: he hadn't been expecting me to do that, and he let me go to catch himself against the wall. As soon as I was free I bolted, heading towards the bedroom at the back of the house, desperate to put another door in between me and Andy.

He cursed and tore after me, catching up too fast because of his long legs, but I just managed to slip into the room and shut the door behind me. Andy's heavy body slammed into the wood just as I engaged the lock. He rattled the doorknob, bellowing in rage, absolutely furious that I'd managed to lock him out. My eyes swiveled around the room, so fast it made me dizzy, as I spun, looking for something I could use. I'd kept my grip on my knife, but like an idiot I'd dropped my purse, so I didn't have a phone on me anymore. I did the only thing I could think to do and hid. I slithered under the bed, trying to scrunch myself up as small as possible.

It took him several minutes, but eventually Andy managed to break the door down, staggering as the flimsy wood failed. I bit my lip hard enough to draw blood, swallowing the whimper that was trying to claw up my throat.

"What the fuck is wrong with you, Anna?" he called, starting to look for me. "Why are you being such a fucking tease?"

I wanted to shout at him, to tell him that if he hated my "teasing" so much he could just fucking leave, but I didn't want to give myself away. I was barely breathing, my heart thundering in my chest, trying desperately to keep quiet. He made a circuit around my bedroom, shoving into the closet and the bathroom, searching for me, and I stopped breathing entirely when he stopped beside the bed.

I saw his weight shift, saw him begin to crouch down like he meant to check under the bed, and I tried to squirm away, my whole body trembling, when a vicious roar tore through the quiet, something that sounded animalistic but like no animal I'd even heard before, full of rage and something else, something bleak and painful. I froze, as did Andy, and then there was a crash, glass shards falling all around the bed, as something crashed through the window that sat above the headboard.

Something heavy landed above me on the bed, its weight pressing the mattress down on top of me, and I heard a snarl, the sound feral and furious.

Andy yelped, falling back on his ass, scurrying to get away from whatever had come through my bedroom window. The glass shards cut into his palms, leaving bloody tracks on the hardwood floors, but he didn't seem to notice, his eyes wide and his breaths panting. Whatever it was crept forward, stepping onto the floor now, and my eyes widened as huge brown paws sank into view, glass crunching under those huge, heavy feet. Whatever it was was still snarling and growling, advancing on Andy slowly, driving him back towards the door.

I was shuddering uncontrollably now, my fingers too numb to properly grip the knife, but even as terror shot through me, making me doubt the control I had on my bladder, a scent rolled over me, achingly familiar but with a wilder tinge I'd never smelled before.

I smelled Chris. I smelled my husband.

As if in a trance, I slid out from under the bed and stood on shaky legs, my knees feeling too liquid to support me, but somehow they did. As soon as I caught sight of what had crashed through my window I gasped, the closed switchblade slipping from my fingers to clatter to the floor. The creature whipped its huge, shaggy head around to look at me, and then I was well and truly frightened.

It was huge, probably as big as some bears, and covered in shaggy dark fur all over most of its body. It walked on all fours, stalking Andy, but it was hunched weirdly, and I caught sight of front paws that looked more like hands, tipped in wickedly-sharp black talons. A mouth overcrowded with needle-sharp teeth was spread wide in a grotesque show of aggression, small pointed ears flat against its huge skull. The nose reminded me a bit of a vampire bat's, the brows so heavy and jutting I had trouble seeing the eyes.

But I *could* see them, if barely. And I knew those eyes.

The creature turned away from me, its attention back on Andy, stalking the terrified man.

"L-leave him alone," I whispered, not wanting to see Andy torn to shreds in front of me. "P-p-please...Chris."

The creature froze, spinning to face me and jumping back up on the bed to snarl in my face. The growling in his chest turned deeper, more furious, but now that he was closer I could smell him: sweet warmth, like being dipped in honey, or biting into fresh-baked bread—Chris.

My body wanted to flee, to run run run and hide away from this thing, this monster, this nightmare made flesh. But my mind refused to let it, held it firm and facing the creature. I lifted my chin, staring him down, searching those eyes I knew so well.

"Chris," I said again, proud of the strength in my voice. "Where the fuck have you been?"

# 3

CHRIS

Pain. Blinding, mind-shattering pain. It was the sort of pain I just knew, on an instinctual level, meant I was dying.

I tried to retrace my steps, to figure out how I'd gotten here, but my mind was so slow, so bogged down by the shredded feel of my body, that I could only conjure faint flashes of images, no more substantial than smoke.

*Dark road slipping by beneath the car, dotted yellow lines blurring into a solid. Trees all around me looming, blinking in and out of existence with the passing of my headlights.*

*The plastic bag on the seat next to me, full of the surprise dessert I'd picked up for Anna when I'd gotten the rest of the groceries. It was chocolate-covered strawberries, her favorite, with a delicate swirling design worked into the tops in pink chocolate that were too pretty to risk mussing them up in the trunk with everything else. I'd just barely stopped myself from buckling the bag in for added security.*

*Something darting out into the road, huge and shaggy and gray, eyes red glowing embers in the nighttime dark.*

*The trees coming closer, too close, jumping out in front of me so fast I couldn't even yell.*

*The screech and crunch of my car crumbling all around me, glass and metal shards slicing into my face, my hands, everywhere.*

*Anna's strawberries sailing through the air to smash into the dashboard, the packaging splitting open and spilling chocolatey berry everywhere. Knew I* should have buckled them in. Anna's gonna be disappointed, *I'd thought.*

My breaths were short and panting, but I couldn't manage to get them any deeper. I didn't know if I was making noises or not, but I wanted to call out, to try and get help. My arms didn't want to move to dig my phone out of my pocket. This road wasn't too remote, so someone would come by eventually, but I had no idea where I'd wound up. If I was far enough back in the trees, it would be morning before someone was able to spot my car.

I couldn't die. I couldn't do that to Anna. She was the light of my life, the most beautiful and generous soul I'd ever met, and she needed me. She was delicate, my Anna, and I knew she struggled a lot more than she let on with the weight of the world, wanting to make everyone but herself happy and comfortable. She needed me to take care of her, 'cause lord knows she wouldn't do it on her own.

*Anna...*

The pain refused to ebb, sweeping my mind away from the here-and-now, from being able to focus on what I needed to do. What I needed to do to get back to Anna.

Tears started to fall, hot like acid on my cheeks, as my arms still refused to work, to grab my phone, to haul my broken body out of the car and drag me to the road. All I could do was moan and try to keep breathing.

*Someone*, I begged, my voice staying locked away in my tight throat. *Help. Someone.*

Through the blind fog of my pain, I heard heavy footsteps approaching. Heavy ones, and the rhythm wasn't quite what I would expect from a person. *An animal?* I thought, my mind still so muddy.

My already shallow breaths picked up speed, getting more desperate and sucking. I couldn't go out like this, mauled by an animal after suffering a car wreck. Anna needed me. *Anna. Baby, I'm so sorry. That thing came out of nowhere and I panicked. I'm so, so sorry baby.*

I heard snuffling at the side of my head, but it was in my blind spot and I couldn't summon the strength to turn to it, to see what I was dealing with. No, there—in the side mirror, dangling loose along the side of the car now, there was a light. Red, like a stop light, but the wrong shape, and dimly I realized that there was no way I was sitting at an angle to catch a traffic light.

My stomach dropped, my skin going icy all in a rush. The animal I'd swerved to avoid, the one like no animal I'd ever seen except in my nightmares, had had red eyes like that.

As if it'd heard me thinking about it the creature began to growl, the sound too deep, too gravelly, clearly coming from a huge and powerful chest, and I realized I was losing control of my bladder, my tears falling harder and hotter. A gray snout packed with needle teeth dipped into my peripheral. I had the vague impression of a canine head sprouting from an impossibly huge body packed with muscle. The creature's growling intensified, turning into vicious snarls that carried the scent of blood and rot.

Quick as lightning, that terrifying maw was opening, needled teeth sinking deep into the meat of my shoulder, tugging *hard*. A strangled sound halfway between a scream and a grunt ripped from my frozen throat, pain searing through me in a fresh wave that almost made me black out. The creature growled into my flesh, long limbs tipped with wicked black talons coming up to brace against the window frame, giving itself leverage.

*Oh god, it's trying to pull me from the car.* Its strong jaw opened just far enough so that the creature could adjust its grip on me, yanking again, and this time I did black out, terror and pain pulling me under.

# 4



<u>CHRIS</u>

When I came to, I was laid out on the forest floor, my clothes shredded and the dripping maw of the creature dipping towards my soft belly with hellish slowness. I had awoken just in time to witness myself being eaten alive by a creature from humanity's collective worst nightmares, and if I'd had the strength I would have screamed. I closed my eyes, willing this to end, for my body to just give out and spare me this torture. *I'm so sorry, Anna. I love you so much. Please know that I would never have left you if I'd had a say in it.*

I didn't even have the strength to brace for it, to try and get away. All I could do was close my eyes and pray I'd die before it got too bad. I'd already lost a lot of blood by the time the thing had found me, and if the raw burning in my shoulder was any indication, it had ripped another huge hole in me when it dragged me from the wreckage.

But the seconds ticked along, and I still didn't feel that needle-crusted mouth tearing into me. My curiosity got the better of me, and I cracked open my eye.

The creature was standing frozen, its hackles raised and its small rounded ears straining forward. It snarled once, snapping at the air, before darting away into the forest.

Which begged the question: what the fuck was coming here that something like that was turning tail?

It was getting harder to breathe, and I felt icy cold everywhere except my ruined shoulder. It had become too difficult to keep my heavy eyelids propped open, so I let them slide closed, hoping that I was finally done with this. I didn't want to leave my Anna, but I was so tired, so scared of what was lurking in these woods, the wider world completely oblivious to its existence.

It wasn't so bad, the dying, now that most of the pain had slipped away and I'd made a kind of peace with it. I conjured thoughts of my wife, of the way her green eyes sparkled whenever she was about to lay into me with one of her ridiculous puns. I brought up the night I'd proposed, both of us soaked and shivering and me without a ring, but she'd looked so goddamn beautiful and perfect, I hadn't been able to stop myself. I recalled her on our wedding day, looking vaguely surprised that we were going through with it, because she always thought I was too good for her. What a lunatic. She hadn't worn white, and I hadn't worn a tux, and we'd gone down to the courthouse like the broke millennials we were, getting married by an apple-faced judge who told us we reminded him of him and his wife, married thirty-five years. I thought of how easy it was to love her, what an honor it had been to hold her through her panic attacks, to rock her through her tears, to light up her face with my clowning around when I saw her start to look haunted and sad. My friends never quite understood why I was so obsessed with her, but that was alright — they didn't need to understand it. All that mattered was that when I looked at her my heart still skipped a beat, my stomach still got fluttery with butterflies, because she was beautiful, and smart, and funny in her dry way, and she made me feel like I could do anything.

Another tear leaked from the corner of my eye, my thoughts turning sluggish and gray. I could feel my heartbeat slowing dangerously, realized my lungs weren't able to pull in any air at all. *I should be dead already*, I thought bitterly. *Why am I still here?*

I felt my heart stop. I felt myself die.

And then I felt myself be reborn.

It was worse than the crash, the pain that ripped along every nerve, stringing me so tight I couldn't get more than creaking whines out, though everything in me wanted to scream. I arched and bowed up off of the forest floor, my silent screams scraping my throat raw, somehow. Or maybe they weren't silent, and I just couldn't hear them. Breath surged back into my lungs, and I felt my heart restart with a sickening lurch.

Then I blacked out again.

This time felt longer, heavier, more clinging. I awoke slowly, instead of all in a rush, and the creature was back, pacing a few feet away and snarling at me. I got to my feet and was shocked to find that I *could*... and that my feet felt different. That *all* of me felt different, my muscles thrumming with strength and my balance shifted so that it felt more comfortable on all fours. I looked down and wanted to faint all over again when I saw a muzzle sprouting from my face. I scrambled back more, flipping onto my back, and got my first glimpse of my new high-ankled feet. My hands were warped, twisted to something in between the hands I was used to and paws, each finger tipped with a long talon just like the creature's.

*What the fuck is happening?*

A high-pitched whine started in my throat, making the creature snarl at me, but it wasn't approaching me, was keeping its distance, and I rolled to my feet and sat on the ground. I was panting, panic making me lightheaded and dizzy, but I tried my best to get my breathing under control, to stop the spiraling in my head, and as I calmed I noticed some things.

First, I could actually see. Being so far from the main road, things had been pretty much pitch-black before, but now I could see the forest around me and the creature that had attacked me as if it was dawn instead of night. I could hear more, too: owls swooping through the trees, nocturnal rodents scurrying through the underbrush, a pair of foxes fighting off in the distance. The strangest one was how my sense of smell had changed; everything smelled different—brighter, sharper, more detailed, and I could smell my own blood on the air not just as a copper tang, but like *me* too. I could scent the creature, the animals downwind of me, the different plants all around me, the asphalt and car smells of the road...and people. I could smell people.

I could hear them too, crashing through the underbrush and calling out. "Hello?" a man's voice echoed in the silence. "Hello? Me and my wife just want to help! We found the wreck and...ah, shit I might as well just call the police." I even heard when he muttered under his breath, "So much damn blood. No way someone survived that."

*I didn't.* I thought, looking down at my terrifying new hands. What the fuck was this? What had happened to me? I looked more like the creature now, I realized, and whipped around to face it with a snarl of my own, but I was alone now, the scent of the creature dimming in the little clearing.

I heard the distant stranger call in the accident and return to his car, and I decided I needed to know, needed to see. I loped back to my car, nausea roiling in my gut, and ripped the dangling side mirror all the way free—something that I should not have been strong enough to do. As I was walking away I saw my phone on the ground, the screen cracked but still functional. I stashed it in what was left of my jeans, then pried the door open so I could grab the portable charger from the glove box. Then I spun and darted off in the direction I smelled water, thirst burning in my throat.

It didn't feel real anymore, what was happening. Clearly I was having one hell of a nightmare and any minute I'd wake up and roll over and pull Anna into my arms, breathing in her sweet smell to calm myself. It was too insane, too ridiculous, that I'd wound up dying on the way home from the grocery store, only to come back as a monster.

I made it to the water—just a trickling little brook tucked into a dip in the land—and drank my fill. The water was crisp and cool, tasting faintly like minerals. Once the burning ache in my throat had eased I brought up the side mirror to take the first real look at my face.

What I saw broke me.

I'd never been a great beauty, but I'd been pretty okay looking, and Anna had even insisted I was handsome. But now no one could possibly call me that, not even Anna.

My face was horrible and twisted, a cruel mockery of a human face that looked like something between a dog and a bat. Needle-sharp teeth just like the thing that had attacked me had crowded out of my mouth, twisting my lips and giving me a permanent snarl. A snout had sprouted from the middle of my face, warping my mouth further, the gaping nostrils no doubt part of why I could smell so well now. No eyebrows, but there was a heavy ridge over my eyes, making them look smaller and beadier. But when I looked closely I saw that my eyes, at least, looked the same. I was covered in shaggy fur the same color as my hair, but certain areas were bare, and my face was one of them. My chest and the upper part of my abdomen was also un-furred, as were my palms and the soles of my feet—paws—whatever.

I started shaking, the horror of my appearance making something inside me snap. I dropped to my knees, threw my head up to the unfeeling night sky, and screamed.

# 5

ANNA

My voice might have been strong, but my body was feeling limp and shivery. A part of me was pretty sure I was hallucinating. How else do you explain a monster bursting into your bedroom to stop a predator from hurting you, only for that monster to wind up being your presumed-dead husband? But I knew what I was seeing, what I was smelling.

"Come on, Chris," I coaxed gently, holding my hand out to him and hoping he'd take it. "Come here. Talk to me. Please." I swallowed around the thick lump in my throat. "Baby, I've missed you so much."

The creature that was Chris shrank back from me, a canine whine slipping out of him. Those bright brown eyes, so soft and warm I hadn't been able to help falling in love with them, were full of a desperate kind of longing, a sadness I wanted to hold him through, like he'd held me so many times.

Andy took Chris' distraction as an opportunity to run, scrambling out of the house and slamming the front door on his way out. I was barely aware of it as I took a tentative step closer to my long-lost spouse. I kept my hand outstretched, my whole body tingling with the desire to touch him, to press my face into his furry neck and breathe that addictive scent of him in deep. I *needed* him, his absence an ache I'd been living with for far too long.

"It's okay, baby," I soothed, taking another shuffling step closer. "It's okay." I wasn't sure if I was telling him or me at this point.

I kept taking small steps closer to him, my hand out and my face soaking wet with the tears that had started falling at some point. But I was also smiling, the only fear in my heart the one that he'd disappear as suddenly as he'd appeared.

"Stay back, Anna," he growled, backing away from me. His voice sounded like he'd been gargling glass and gravel, but I still recognized it. And he knew my name. He knew me. He remembered me. I could fly, I was so happy and relieved.

I stopped my advance, but kept my hand out and straining towards him. "Why?" I asked, bringing my other hand up and opening my arms wide. "Come here. Please. I need you—"

"You *need* to stay far away from me!" he roared, his hackles raising. I flinched, my arms lowering a fraction. "I'm too dangerous. Too...you need to stay away from me."

I cocked my head. "Too what?"

"Nevermind."

I frowned at him, dropping my arms and putting my fists on my hips instead. "You've been missing for almost a year. The fucking *least* you can do is tell me what happened. Though I would prefer you get your furry ass over here and let me hug you, you stubborn bastard."

It was hard to read the expression on his new face, but the shock and disbelief were easier to see in his eyes. I didn't usually talk to him like that, but I was at the end of my rope.

"Why aren't you freaking out right now?" he said in a low voice that was soft with incredulity. "I'm a goddamn *monster*, Anna."

I shrugged. "You're also Chris. The man I've had to declare dead and live without for almost a year despite feeling, in my soul, that he was still alive. The man who said he'd never leave me, that he'd love me forever. The man who I swore to love until the end of my days, in sickness and in health, 'til death do us part. And baby, you look different but you don't look dead."

He blinked at me, then edged carefully closer, almost like he was doing it against his will. "This isn't just sickness, love," he rasped. "This is...so much worse."

I studied his new face, at the mouth now straining closed around the teeth crowded in there, at the deadly claws tipping his hands. I looked at his cute little pointed ears, flicked back against his head, at the shaggy fur the same molasses brown his hair had been. I took in the snoutlike nose with its large flaring nostrils, and I just...didn't care. I shrugged again.

"Worse would be if you were dead. Or if you didn't remember me. I mean, it'll be an adjustment of course, but I really don't care, Chris. I just want you. I *need* you. Please come here and hold me."

He looked torn, his body so tense he was vibrating. I swallowed and held my arms back out, begging him with my eyes to come to me, to make me feel whole again.

We were both silent for several heartbeats, the only sound in the room our loud breaths and the night sounds trickling in from the broken window. Somewhere out there someone took a corner too hard, tires squealing, and that sound broke whatever fragile spell had been holding us; before I could blink Chris was spinning away from me, his rangy limbs eating up the distance between himself and the broken window. I heard the bedsprings creak, heard broken glass tinkle, and then the shaggy wolfish monster who had been my husband was gone.

"No!" I heard myself scream, my feet crunching shards of glass under my work shoes as I tried to follow him. "Chris, please! Come back!" I scrambled up onto the bed and stuck my head out of the window, glass splinters biting into my flesh. "*Chris!*"

But the backyard was empty, everything still and quiet, mocking me and my desperate tears.

# 6

CHRIS

I cursed myself over and over for my foolishness, my weakness. Anna was beyond my reach now, no matter how badly I wanted her, no matter what insanity was making her say that she still wanted me.

My phone started vibrating in my tattered pocket, and I drew up, clawing it out and looking at the display with a pained groan. Anna was calling, the picture from our wedding I used as her contact photo filling the cracked screen. I held it in my shaking hand, torn about what to do, until it went to voicemail. But instead of leaving a message like she would have before, she immediately called again, and this time I declined the call and shoved it back into my pocket. I knew what she was doing, and I wasn't going to give in that easily. She wasn't in her right mind, likely in shock from what had happened with that asshole and seeing me like this. Once she'd slept on it she'd feel differently.

How could she not?

My phone kept ringing, over and over again, as I loped back to the small cave—really more like a hollow in the ground—that I had turned into my home. It was close to our house, so I could keep an eye on Anna, protect her, but far enough away that our neighbors wouldn't just stumble on me. It was risky as fuck being this close to people, especially knowing so many of our neighbors were hunters, but I couldn't leave her. Not just because she needed me, but because I needed her.

My friends used to tease me that we were co-dependent, but I'd never given a shit. It was mutual, and we weren't so entangled in each other that we abandoned everyone else. We'd just always known that the other person was the star at the center of our lives.

Fuck, it was so hard to walk away from her. To turn my back on her begging me, pleading with me to stay. It was such a small thing, to just *not leave,* but it wouldn't have been responsible to do that. Wouldn't have been right, because it would have been selfish.

I tucked myself into the nest of shredded fabric I'd crafted into my bed, finally giving in to the urge to check my phone now that I was hidden.

*23 missed calls,* my screen read. I gulped, unlocking the phone and seeing that I also had three new voicemails and several texts.

I should just ignore it all. I should get rid of the fucking thing, cut that last tie and move on for real, find someplace else to haunt for a while. But my clawed thumb was sliding over to the voicemail notification and I couldn't stop it.

*"Chris you absolute bastard, come back here and fucking talk to me! You owe me that, to at least talk to me like an adult. With everything we've been through it's the least I deserve!"*

I swallowed, my throat feeling dry and aching. *"Please, Chris, baby,"* the next message started, her voice so hollow and hopeless it felt like my heart was collapsing in on itself. *"Please, I miss you so much. Please just come back and see me. Please talk to me. Please, please, please..."* Her voice faded away on a tear-soaked whine, and it felt like I was dying all over again, knowing I'd done that. I'd made her sound like that.

The last voicemail was largely the sound of her crying and trying to choke out words, and it was so tortured and heartbreaking I was crying right along with her, my faith in my decision slipping. "You better come back here," she gasped out. "Or I swear to god I'm going to go looking for you. I'm not losing you again." Then she hung up, and that was it.

Blinking to try and clear my blurred vision, I fumbled my way over to the texts next. It was more of the same: *come back, let me talk to you, please I miss you.*

My heart was raw and aching in my chest, my limbs all tight with shame and hurt. She was right, I did at least owe her an explanation. I owed her the world, but I could give her this.

*I'm sorry, Anna. I wish it didn't have to be like this, but you understand why I can't just come back, don't you?*

The three dots popped up immediately, making me feel even lower. *No, I don't. I want you back, you want to be back, so what's the problem?*

Maybe she hadn't gotten a good look at me. It was hard to remember how my vision had been before. Maybe it had been too dark for her to really see me. *I can't just be Chris anymore,* I insisted. *Chris is dead, sweetheart. I'm just a monster stuck with his memories.*

*Do you wish you couldn't remember me, then? That you didn't remember us?*

I squeezed my eyes shut, a whine slipping out of my throat. As much as it tortured me to remember those good times, to pine for what was lost, I knew with everything in me that I didn't want that. *If anything I wish you didn't remember me,* I sent.

She tried calling again, and this time I was so turned around and brittle that I picked up, pressing the phone to my face and saying nothing.

"Thank you for picking up this time," she said, and if she'd meant it to be sarcastic it hadn't managed to come out that way. "I can't begin to imagine what it would be like to adjust to what happened to you, but I promise it doesn't bother me. Doesn't that count for something?"

"You're in shock," I growled, closing my eyes and letting her soft voice wash over me. "It was dark. You didn't get a good look at me."

She sighed, her breath sounding like static through the phone connection. "You can think that all you want but I got a pretty good look. The lamp was on." I blinked, trying to think back. Had it been? Or had it only been the light from the backyard floodlamp? "Do you not trust me anymore, baby?" she asked softly.

"Of course I do," I said without hesitation. I'd trust her with my life, with anything. But this was different, wasn't it?

She sighed in my ear, sounding frustrated now more than sad. "There isn't anything I can say that will convince you, is there?"

"I don't know," I answered honestly. I knew Anna wouldn't lie to me, but she'd been known to lie to herself. That was a big part of what her chronic anxiety and depression were, after all: one part of her brain lying to the rest of it.

My phone chimed in my ear, and I saw that she was requesting a video call with me. "Accept it, Chris," she told me, voice hard. I didn't want to, but her voice brooked no argument, and whenever she got bossy like that…I turned into a puddle.

I accepted, but not before turning the brightness all the way down so that my face would be that much harder to see. To my surprise, Anna was bright-eyed and appeared to be naked, her green eyes boring into the camera. "Turn the brightness up, you cheater," she said with a stern look. "I want to see your face."

I barked a harsh laugh. "No, you don't."

"Don't tell me what I want," she snapped, angling the phone so I could see that she was, indeed, naked and sprawled out on our stripped-down bed. "I want to see my husband while I touch myself," she purred, her free hand sliding down her body, tugging at her peaked brown nipple and making herself gasp. "Don't you want to give me what I want, Chris?"

I gulped, my throat dry and my cock surging to life so fast it hurt. I wanted to keep protesting, to keep fighting off this beautiful, clearly insane woman for her own good...but I was weak. I was selfish.

I wanted her so, so bad.

I did as she asked, sliding the brightness higher until my face was more or less visible in the little preview window in the corner. A bright smile stretched across her pretty face, her eyes going bright and glassy. "There you are," she breathed, looking at me with so much tenderness and love it ached. "Thank you, baby. What do you want me to do first?"

"I-it's all good. I want you to do what feels good." I'd love anything she gave me.

"If you were here in the room with me, what would you want to do first?"

That was an easy answer; it was the same thing I always wanted to do to her when we tumbled into bed. "I'd...I'd bury my face between those sexy legs of yours and eat that gorgeous pussy." I shifted in my nest, pressing the palm of my free hand into my dick throbbing away in my pants. I rocked my hips into the pressure, my breath coming faster.

Anna moaned, lifting her arm and tilting her phone so she could still see me on the screen, but I could see her hand sliding down her belly, her fingers combing through the thatch of curls over her mound until she hit the part in her pussy lips. She dipped into her slit, just for a second, then brought her fingers up so I could see them, see how shiny and wet they were with her arousal. "You see that?" she asked huskily, bringing the phone down so that I was up close and personal with the cunt that had ruined me for all other cunts the moment I'd tasted it. "You see how wet I am for you? How much you turn me on?" I whimpered, my hand pressing harder into my shaft as I continued rocking my hips.

"I see it, baby," I rasped, teeth gnashing as I struggled to keep control of my body. Fuck, I missed her. I missed her scent, her taste, the way she screamed her pleasure but whispered love and praise into my ear while we made love, as if she wanted the world to know how well I fucked her but wanted only me to know how well she loved me. I missed her laughter, her corny jokes, the way she'd tuck herself tight against me when she needed me to talk her down from the edge of a panic attack. "What are you going to do with that sweet, juicy cunt of yours?" I asked, breathless with need for my wife.

"I'm going to touch myself," she promised, bringing the phone back up so that she was back to being able to see me on the screen. "And I'm going to look at you the entire time I do it."

True to her word, Anna's hand started working furiously between her legs, the flesh of her thighs jumping and quivering as her pleasure started to grow. Her head tilted back, exposing more of her throat, and I felt the sudden overwhelming urge to bite her there, to sink my teeth into that smooth stretch of delicate skin until she'd be wearing my mark, more permanent than the rings we'd exchanged. She trembled and whined, biting her lip, but she never looked away, never closed her eyes for longer than it took to blink, and as her cries grew louder, her peak surging to swallow her up, I felt my own release burning down my spine, making my legs shiver and cramp as I pressed my hand desperately against the too-sensitive skin of my now monstrous cock. I slipped myself past the waistband of my tattered jeans, pulling the fabric down as far as it would go, as Anna froze, going still and quiet, before she came with a guttural cry, her hips bucking up and her legs snapping closed. I squeezed the new strange knot at the root of my dick and followed her soon after, hot seed splashing all over the rags of my bedding, my hand, my belly, making me moan and twitch with each spurt from my pulsing cock.

We both lay there panting, staring at each other through the phone screen, for several long minutes.

"Come home, Chris," Anna said again softly, sitting up and pointing the screen more fully at her face. She looked tired now, sleepy from her long day and her orgasm. "Please come home."

I hesitated, a hundred reasons why I shouldn't, why I should stay away dancing on my tongue. But she'd looked at me the whole time, just like she'd said. She'd looked at me and she still wanted me.

"Alright," I agreed, feeling every inch like the monster I was. "I'll come back tomorrow night. So we can talk. You're right, I do owe you that." Anna smiled.

"Thank you," she said, grinning sleepily. "I'll see you tomorrow night. I love you, Chris. I've missed you so, so much."

"I love you, too, Anna. I missed you too. Of course I did. Look at you."

With another soft smile she ended the call, and I used the soiled rags to clean myself up. I couldn't shake the belief that this was going to be a mistake...but my heart also couldn't shake that it felt right.

# 7

ANNA

Obviously I couldn't go in to work the next day. If my husband coming back from the dead as a strange werewolf-like creature wasn't grounds for using a personal day then I didn't know what was. Plus if I went in I'd have to see Andy and all that that entailed, and I just didn't have the mental bandwidth to even think about that.

I slept on the couch, too tired to clean up all of the glass from our bedroom, but once I woke up the next morning I did my best to tackle it, glad that I would have a couple of clear days before I had to worry about rain. An irrational part of me was demanding I leave the broken window uncovered, waiting for Chris' return. I didn't want him to have any doubts about whether or not he was welcome.

It was strange for me to be the calm one, the sure one. It might have been the first time in our long and beautiful relationship that I was the one having to settle and soothe him, to ease his insecurities and anxieties instead of the other way around. But it felt doable; I had so much experience being on the receiving end of comfort that I felt like I knew what I needed to do to help him. Plus he may look different, but at his core he was still the man I married, and I could let that fact guide me.

I tried my best to keep myself busy with cleaning and getting ready. I wanted everything to be perfect for my date tonight, but more so I had to pass the sluggish hours until sundown, and all the nervous energy thrumming through me demanded I do something physical.

I kept thinking about last night, how good it had felt to feel that connection with him again, even through the phone. It had been so fucking hot, putting on a show for him, watching him lose control and come for me despite himself. Even though his features looked different, I'd been thrilled to recognize his O-face, to see that proof that he wasn't really all that different now. Every time the memories flooded in it made me want to touch myself all over again, but I wanted to hold off and save all of that energy for tonight. I had a reluctant were-husband to seduce, after all.

Finally it began to approach sundown, my heart pounding harder and harder in my chest as night drew closer. I hadn't been able to resist texting him periodically during the day, but he hadn't responded, and I hoped it was because he was nocturnal now and not because he was having second thoughts. Once the sun had begun to set below the tree line my phone finally buzzed with a text.

*I dreamed about you,* he sent to me, making me break out in a big goofy grin. *Usually it would make me sad but knowing I'm going to see you again soon makes it all better.* After a second he started typing again. *I shouldn't be letting you talk me into this. It's not responsible. You deserve so much more than I can give you now.*

I grinned at my phone. *Keep it coming, I'm eating it up. Also you're not the boss of me, I can decide for myself what I want and what I deserve XP.*

*:) Yes ma'am.*

I giggled and squealed like I was back in high school talking to my first boyfriend, hugging my phone to my chest and doing my best to contain my excitement so I could finish getting myself ready for him.

Once it was fully dark I went into the bedroom to wait for him, sitting on the bed and playing puzzle games on my phone to distract myself until I heard a cautious rustling in the backyard. I scrambled onto my knees to peer out into the night, cursing my weak eyes for not being able to see him in the shadows.

"Chris?" I called out softly, my eyes roving.

"You didn't cover the window?" he asked from right below me. I sucked in a breath, my eyes finally able to pick him out now that I'd heard him.

"I wanted you to be able to get back in!" I told him as I backed away to give him room to climb inside. "Something told me you wouldn't want to use the front door."

Chris leaped up and grabbed onto the window ledge, the deadly sharp claws of his hands digging into the wood. I heard his back feet scrabbling up the brick on the outside, and then he was hoisting his huge form up and through the window. He dropped onto the bed and shot me a look when a piece of glass fell onto the floor from wherever it had been hiding. I sighed, rolling my eyes.

"I changed the sheets and vacuumed in here at least three times, how is there *still* glass?" I huffed, suddenly tense now that he was here. He'd left so abruptly last night, going from looking like he was right there with me to bolting in the space of a breath.

I edged closer to him, letting some distance remain between us even though every cell in my body was begging me to take a running leap at him.

He was skittish. I had to respect that if I wanted him to stay this time.

"So you're not dead," I said, grinning. "I get why you felt like you couldn't come back, but where have you been this whole time?"

He looked uncomfortable, hunching in on himself and avoiding my eyes. "Close," he hedged. "I didn't want to leave you alone and vulnerable so I've been trying to keep an eye on you." He looked up at me then, concern furrowing his heavy brow. "You've really got to be more careful on your walks, Anna. You know it's not safe, and with me gone…"

"But you're not really gone," I pointed out, all of the times that I'd felt him near, that I could have sworn I'd caught the scent of his skin and dismissed it as wishful thinking running through my mind. I'd never really been alone these last months, and even if I was mad he stayed away I understood why he'd done it, and the fact that he'd stuck around to try and protect me softened me. "You're still here and we still want each other."

Then I couldn't take it anymore: I closed the last of the distance between us and threw my arms around his neck, holding onto him for dear life. Because that's exactly what he was to me: dear life, the other half of me, my true home. I didn't care what he looked like, just so long as he was still *mine*.

He snarled in my ear, holding himself stiff, refusing to touch me, but as I began to sob into his neck and squeeze him tight he softened, his long furry arms wrapping me up tight and holding me close, rocking me and burying his face in my hair. He gasped out my name, those new claws of his prickling into my skin just the littlest bit, but it didn't hurt, it only made my skin tingle and flush. I tried to press myself in closer, hating every inch of empty space still between our bodies. As our pelvises crashed together, I felt his cock stirring in the tattered remains of his jeans.

I sucked in a breath, sliding my hips in a circle so I'd brush up against him again. He sucked in a breath, his arms going tighter around me, one arm sliding down to cup my ass, guiding me in more firmly against his hardening cock.

"*Anna*," he snarled as my hands started exploring his new body, combing through the fur to stroke the hard slabs of lean muscle beneath. I pressed my breasts into his chest, moaning at the spirals of pleasure that sweet friction sent curling through my belly. He groaned, pressing his face into my neck again and breathing deep. "How can you still want me?" he asked softly even as he grabbed my hips and ground my sex onto his throbbing erection.

"I didn't marry you for your looks, baby," I panted into his soft-looking ear. "I married you because you're you. And I'll *never* not want you." His hips bucked against me, his cock rock hard and straining against the already struggling fabric still clinging to him. I pulled back, looking him in the eyes. "I've had to go without you for months. I need you, Chris. I need you *now*." I cupped his face in my hands and brought it down closer to mine. "Maybe we'll have to get creative with some things now but I don't give a shit." I paused, bracing to ask the question I was most scared of, "Do you want me to stop?"

He studied me for a long moment, his limbs shivering slightly, then shook his head, his lips quivering over his sharp teeth.

I dragged him down the rest of the way and kissed him, his mouth a mix of strange and familiar. I sighed, my arms wrapping around his neck again, keeping him pinned against me. His arms pulled me in snug, hauling me up so he didn't have to hunch, and I wrapped my legs around his waist instinctively. It was hard for him to kiss me with his lips already so stiff around his teeth, and there was no way I was sticking my tongue in his mouth unless we sanded those things down somehow, but his tongue still worked fine. Better than fine, actually; it felt longer than it had been, more mobile, and I whimpered into his mouth as he swept it against mine. Chris had always been a certified expert at eating pussy, and I was breathless imagining the things he could do to me with that tongue.

He started walking with me towards the bed, but stopped and looked at the rumpled bedspread suspiciously.

"Probably not safe," he growled, making me laugh.

"I don't care where you take me so long as you stuff me full of that glorious cock right this minute," I told him, nipping at his lower lip.

# 8

<u>CHRIS</u>

It wasn't possible. I had to be dreaming, because there was no way Anna would see me like this and still want me. I'd convinced myself that last night had been a fluke and all we'd do is talk. I'd give her some closure, maybe encourage her to start dating again and forget all about me.

I knew how I looked now. I hadn't been able to stop looking at myself for the longest time, a small part of me hoping desperately that the next time when I looked at myself I'd see the face I was used to, my human face.

But here was Anna, her green eyes wide and full of so much love it made me ache, as if this hideous face was all that she'd ever wanted to see. Her fingers combed through the fur covering my lower stomach, trailing towards the waistband of the filthy scraps of denim I was still wearing even after several months. I grabbed her wrist just before she got there, careful not to hurt her with my sharp claws. "Anna," I ground out, searching her eyes—for what, I didn't know. "Are you sure? You don't have to do this. I understand. I know what I look like."

Her eyes narrowed, thick dark brows pulling together and wrinkling her pale gold skin. "So do I. I can see you right now," she murmured. "I thought you were dead, Chris." I tried not to flinch. In my mind I *was* dead, in a way. "I don't know how many times I'm going to have to keep saying it, but I'll repeat it as much as I need to until you get it through your thick skull that I don't care. Maybe I should, but I just...don't. You're here. That's all I care about."

I swallowed, my heart hammering in my chest. It was too good to

31

be true. Months of following her around, haunting her like a ghost, convinced she'd freak out and run in horror—and I could have come home any time. She'd been waiting. She still wanted me.

I hefted her up in my arms again, frowning at how much weight she'd lost since I'd last held her, hauling her up and turning around so that she was pressed up against the wall, my body caging her in tight. Her eyes went wide, her pupils blowing and her breaths panting from between her slack lips. I felt her grind herself into me again, and my last shred of control snapped.

I ripped the rags from my body with a snarl, tossing them into a corner. I didn't even flinch when the phone still tucked into the pocket hit the wood floor with a heavy *thunk*. My throbbing cock speared up into the space between us, wet with the lubrication it naturally produced now. It was smoother after the change, a raw red color that still unsettled me, and when I wasn't hard it tucked itself away into a hairy sheath. There was a knot of flesh near the base of it that seemed to collect my spend while I was working myself, and I'd only come when I wrapped my hand around it and squeezed it tight. I didn't know how things could possibly work with Anna with that thing on there, but if she really wanted me then I was helpless but to give her what she wanted.

"I missed you so much, baby," I told her, the fires of my lust giving way to the agony of these last several months. I hadn't been able to stay away from her, even though I knew it would have been better if I had. I'd watched her as she went on her walks, watched her shuffle around the house. I'd heard her cry herself to sleep, sobbing my name and ripping my monstrous heart out of my chest. I'd almost revealed myself to her several times, desperate to soothe her, but the sight of my reflection in the glass had always stopped me. I hadn't been able to face her reaction to me—or at least, what I'd *thought* her reaction would be. The most I'd let myself do was murmur the things I wanted her to know while she was thinking, hoping that somehow she'd know them.

I'd lived for the texts and voicemails she'd sent me every night. They kept me going, gave me something to look forward to, to dream about. My chest squeezed tight as the full reality of her soft and wet and eager in my arms hit me.

I'd thought I'd never get to feel this again. With a growl I slid my long tongue out from between my horrible teeth and slipped it between hers, shuddering and moaning as the familiar sweetness of her burst on my tongue. She tasted like heaven, my own personal salvation, and if she wanted me she was going to get me.

"I missed you, too," she gasped, cupping my face in her hands. "Now fuck me. Please, I need my husband to fill me up like only he does."

I snarled again, baring my teeth, as I sank my claws into the fabric of her blouse and yanked down, careful of her skin. The material split like wet paper, baring her smooth skin to my hungry gaze and making my mouth water. The scent of her had gone deeper, sweeter, headier, and as I ripped away the last of her clothes I realized I was smelling her arousal, the fragrance of her cunt drifting thickly in the cool air of our bedroom. I groaned, dipping my head to nuzzle her throat, fighting to get control of my body. I didn't want to lose control and hurt her.

I'd die if I hurt her.

Her hands slid down between us, trailing over my chest and down my tense abs until her dainty little fingers found the hot throb of my shaft, stroking me roughly, desperately, like she never had before, but I loved it, wanted more of it. My head fell back, hips twitching to follow her sinful little hands, each rough stroke making my knees weak. I whimpered as she squeezed my knot, bringing me perilously close to spilling. I grabbed her hand to stop her, not ready for this to be over yet.

She grinned at me, hunger burning in her eyes. "You have a new toy for me to play with," she breathed, licking her lips. Then she was wrapping her arms around my neck and wriggling up my body until my cock prodded at her sopping wet entrance.

Whatever doubts I'd still been harboring about whether or not she really wanted me fled. There was no way she was faking *that*.

Normally I'd take my time with her, work her up into a fever pitch with my tongue and my fingers and our toys before I ever got near her, but it had been months and we were both far too desperate to go that slow. I grabbed onto her ass and guided her all the way onto me, the weeping head of my cock sinking into her. Anna cried out, her head falling back as she broke out in a wide grin.

"Goddamn, I missed this," she rasped, her eyes rolling up into her head as I let gravity sink her down onto me up to my knot. I shuddered at the feel of her, so familiar and yet still as incredible as if it was the first time.

"Me too," I groaned, adjusting my grip on her so I could start pumping into her. "I'm sorry I stayed away. I didn't think—" I swallowed around the lump in my throat, my chest heaving from a strange combination of lust and pain. She bit her lip, leaning forward so that her forehead pressed to mine, our panting breaths mingling as she worked herself onto me, making us both groan.

"Never leave me again," she begged, her voice tight as her pleasure mounted. "I can't survive without you, and I don't care how unhinged that sounds. Oh fuck, oh *Chris!*" Her lips pressed into a hard line, her eyes squeezing shut with pleasure as I pumped my hips into her tight heat.

"I won't," I promised her with a groan. "Never." I was close now, but I knew without her on my knot I'd get no closer, that I'd be stuck in this achingly hard state until tight pressure wrapped around it. "Can you take my knot, love?" I asked her, searching her green eyes. She nodded, her face flushed and shining with sweat. "That's my good girl," I grinned, snuffling at her hair and licking and nibbling at her sensitive throat as I changed the angle of our hips to try and make this easier for her.

She was absolutely dripping for me, but I knew the stretch would still be a lot, and I didn't want to hurt her. "Give it to me, baby," she gasped, her brows going tight with her looming orgasm. Who was I to deny her when she asked so prettily? With a grunt I drove her down onto my length, forcing my knot past her entrance, hearing it slip inside her with a wet pop. She sucked in a breath, her spine snapping straight, and I froze, watching her closely.

"Are you alright?" I asked, sinking back onto my haunches, my wife still impaled on my cock, then sat down on my ass as carefully as I could so that I could touch more of her. I combed my claws through her hair, stroked her face with the pads of my fingers, trailed my palms over her back and sides. "Anna?"

She nodded, looking at me with a dazed expression. "Yeah. Yeah, I'm fine. It was just a lot." She chuckled, one hand cupping the side of my face. "I'm okay, really. You look like you're going to start freaking out, though."

I shook my head, trying my best to kiss her with my fucked up mouth. She hummed in pleasure and rolled her hips, fucking herself gently on my cock.

The sensation of my knot inside her was unreal, so good I thought surely I wasn't going to survive so much pleasure, my orgasm barreling through me with the force of a volcano. "Fuck, baby," I ground out, my voice filled with gravel, "I'm not going to last much longer. You feel so fucking good."

She bit her lip again and nodded. "You do too. Fuck—the knot, i-it's —" her head sank back, exposing the graceful line of her throat, baring it to me like an invitation. My hips picked up speed and strength so that I was pounding into her, rutting her like the wild beast I now was, my hideous face buried where her shoulder met her neck, breathing her scent in like it was the only thing that would save my life in that moment.

Her orgasm clenched my knot tight like a fist, surprising both of us with its suddenness, and then I was following right after her, the pleasure boiling up from my toes and down my spine, sweet fire sweeping over every nerve in my body as my aching length grew impossibly harder inside her and started firing into her fluttering heat. I could hear myself snarling and crying out, but my body felt strangely distant now, the pleasure whiting out my vision and sending my mind far, far away.

Some instinct took over me then, and I latched onto the meat of her shoulder, right where I'd had my face pressed, my sharp teeth sinking into her tender flesh until I tasted the cocktail of her blood and her sweat on my tongue, sweetened by the flavor of her skin. She sucked in a breath, then I felt her clenching on my cock, another orgasm sweeping her away with so much force she was screaming in my ear.

When I finally stopped coming I loosened my jaw and licked at the shallow wound. It took me a few seconds to realize what had happened, what I'd done, and then I reared back, horror making me cold.

"Fuck. Fuck, no, Anna I—I'm sorry. I—" My softening cock slipped out of her with a rush of hot fluid, and I lowered her to the ground and backed away, wanting to escape what I'd just done to my sweet, beautiful wife. "What have I done?" I moaned, my hands coming up to claw at my face.

# 9

ANNA

I'd never tell him, but I always thought Chris was completely adorable whenever he'd freak out about something. And even with his new face, his new (completely delicious) body, he was just as precious as he always was.

He'd bit me while in the throes of passion, and if my guess was right then I'd be turning into the same kind of creature as him.

I couldn't wait.

The more I looked at him, the more I actually liked the way he looked. He was still my Chris, the warm and beautiful soul that I'd married, but now there was an edge to him, something that wasn't quite dangerous, but definitely wilder, more unfettered, and I liked it. A lot. Sex between us had always been good, but what had just happened was on a whole other level. The sharp pang and burn from him forcing his knot into me had been something I would never have guessed I'd be into, but once the shock had worn off it had caused my pleasure to rocket up to new and exciting heights. And once he'd started moving, and that knot had started pressing right into my g-spot...

I was a goner, and I didn't think I'd ever get enough.

But with Chris now looking the way he did, our old life wasn't going to be an option. And I wasn't going to be able to survive on my own all that much longer, financially. Thanks to Chris' excellent budgeting we'd had enough savings that I'd been alright paying for everything with my minimum-wage income these past months, but even with working some overtime I'd had to dip into the savings a lot, and I think I would have only had another couple of months to figure out what I was going to do next. I'd been thinking about it for months, and no matter what it looked like I'd have to either get a second job or sell the house and car.

But if I was a creature like him, then none of that mattered anymore. We could do like we'd always joked and go feral and live off in the woods.

I noticed that Chris was hurting himself in his panic, and my amusement fled me as quickly as it had sprung up. "Hey, stop that!" I cried, lunging for him and grabbing his wrists. "You're bleeding."

His beady eyes had gone wide, his stretched-out lips trembling against his teeth. "What have I done?" he whispered, looking anguished. "What...what have I..."

I forced his hands away from his face and squeezed them. "You didn't do anything wrong, Chris," I told him soothingly, rubbing my thumbs over his knobby knuckles. "I'm fine. We'll figure it out."

He blinked at me, looking almost like he was mad at me. "*Figure it out? Anna, I bit you. Do you know what that means?*" He spat the words at me, his whole body shivering now, and if I didn't know him so well my temper would have flared at his tone. But this was just another stage of his panic.

"I'm going to turn into what you are," I said quietly, giving him a small smile and scooting closer. "It won't be easy, I'll give you that. It'll be an adjustment, figuring out where we'll live and how we'll survive, but we'll be together. So it'll just be another Anna-and-Chris Adventure, right?"

His chest was heaving with his shallow breaths, making me worried. "Adventure?"

"Yeah. Like when we road-tripped to ComicCon that one time."

He barked a laugh. "Anna, my love, this is nothing like that. I've... I've *ruined* you."

I sighed, dropping his hands so I could force my way into his lap. "Usually I'm the one with the freakouts," I told him, burrowing into his chest whether he liked it or not. "So I'm not sure what I'm supposed to do here. But I feel like this is the point where if the roles were reversed you'd tell me to do my breathing exercises and start talking it out."

He gave a half-hearted chuckle that was almost more of a grunt, but after a moment he relaxed a little bit and cuddled me closer to his body. I combed my fingers through his fur, intrigued by the texture, which was somehow soft and wiry all at once. "My brave, beautiful Anna. I'd be lost without you," he murmured, pressing his face into the top of my head.

"We can't change it," I told him, closing my eyes so I could focus on the intoxicating rhythm of his heart beating against my cheek. "And I don't think I'd want to even if I could. So all we can do is move forward, and I'm excited by it. It's a little scary too, but we'll be together, so it's basically impossible for it to break completely bad." He huffed a laugh and pressed a clumsy kiss into my hair. "I...I wasn't going to last that much longer without you anyway."

"Anna," he groaned, wrapping me up tight in his long, rangy arms. "How are you so calm about this?"

"I don't know," I shrugged. "But stop looking this gift horse in the mouth, you lunatic." After a pause, I hesitantly asked, "So...what do I have to look forward to? How much longer...?"

He sighed, guiding my face up to look at him with a clawed finger. "I don't know. I was already dying because of my injuries from the car crash when the thing got to me and bit me. I don't know if you have to die for the change to take place but...I was human, then I died, and then I was...this."

I felt my eyes widen. "Whoa, spooky."

He sighed, then dropped his hand so he could trail his hand up and down my thigh, making my skin pebble. "We should get you cleaned up then maybe we can...prepare."

I poked him in his concave belly. "Stop being such a downer. Repeat after me: we're together, and we'll figure it out."

He grinned, grabbing my hand when I went to poke him again. "So bossy. Alright: we're together, and we'll figure it out."

# 10



<u>ANNA</u>

My nostrils flared, the familiar scent of my husband joining the bouquet of smells that made up our new home: dust, crisp pine, and woodsmoke tangled up with a smell I could only describe as the wild. I didn't like him leaving me all day, the wound of his yearlong absence still tender even after months of being reunited, but someone had to stay home with the kids, and since I hated hunting it was only natural that it be me.

We'd stumbled on a pair of kittens not long after settling into our tiny cottage in the deep woods—two girls, both tuxedos. We weren't sure if they'd survive the night, but we kept them wrapped up tight and tucked close against us, feeding them round the clock. In the absence of human children, we poured everything we had into those two delicate lives, hoping they'd make it and become ours, our babies. And by some miracle, they'd both pulled through, so we'd named them Belle and Elisa, after two other women who'd fallen in love with monsters.

Chris was not amused, but I insisted.

"There's my girls," he rasped as he slipped through the heavy front door. "How were things while I was out?" I stoked the fire burning low in the hearth and helped him spit the dressed kills for roasting.

"Quiet," I sighed, rubbing my cheek into his furred shoulder. "Missed you."

He kissed the top of my head, his chest rumbling. "Missed you too, sweetheart." I melted at his sweetness.

I'd changed from Chris's bite, but I hadn't changed as much as him. Maybe it was because I'd been healthy when I was bitten, or because I was female, or maybe for some other reason neither of us could have guessed. Everywhere other people could see easily I looked the same, more or less.

But I wasn't the same: I was faster and stronger, my senses and my teeth much sharper now. I didn't need to eat or sleep as much, but I needed more water than I had before. My fur was much finer and more sparse than Chris', and only in areas I could cover with clothes, like my thighs and back. It allowed me to occasionally slip into town for supplies while we were still figuring out this homesteading thing.

Selling our house and the car had been enough to buy a plot of land with a rundown little hunting cabin on it up north and enough construction materials to fix it up and make it livable. It meant leaving a paper trail, but we decided it was worth it to know that we wouldn't be surprised by land development or campers. I sold off most of our stuff before going off the grid, and while it wasn't a *ton* of cash it was enough to sustain us like this for several years if we were careful.

It was rough living, but in a weird way I'd never been happier. I had my best friend back, two soft furry babies to take care of, and I didn't have to worry about trudging into an office to waste forty or more hours of my life every week. I could put in work on a thing and actually see the benefits from that work, wrought with my own two hands, and that process brought so much unexpected joy.

My depression and anxiety were both much better than I could ever remember them being as an adult. Chris teased that it was very "me" that the situation which would make most people more anxious and upset was making me feel better, and I had to agree with him: it *was* kind of funny, when you put it like that.

Once dinner was set up to cook I bumped my shoulder into his and slid my hand down to grab one of his sinfully round ass cheeks, kneading the furred flesh hard enough to make him jump.

He growled in my ear, his tongue tickling the shell of my now-pointed ear when he licked it. "So it was *that* kind of missing, huh?" he growled, his own hand trailing along my side.

I spun, pressing myself into his hard warm body, nipping gently at his chest with my sharp teeth. "Isn't it always?" I purred, arching a brow at him. Another side effect of the transformation—or maybe of just being in a better place mentally—was that I was hornier than I'd ever been, hungry for him constantly in a way that I couldn't seem to ignore. I stepped back, giving myself enough room to slip my hands between us so I could peel my smock dress off of myself.

Chris started rumbling deep in his chest, stepping into the space I'd made and wrapping his arms around me with a snarl that made the heat and wetness pooling between my thighs intensify. He dipped his head, snuffling at my neck and skimming his own teeth along the delicate skin at my pulse point, making me shiver and whimper. "I live to serve, sweet Anna," he whispered, his clawed hands cupping my breasts, hefting them as his thumbs flicked the nipples gently. "Just tell me what you need, love." I pressed into his touch, my breaths panting with my need, but I was craving something else tonight. Something more…wild.

"I-I need…" my breath hitched as he slid one hand further down my body, dipping the pad of one clawed finger into my wet folds and circling the aching throb of my clit. "I need you…to catch me." I shoved myself away from him, using my new strength to break his hold and bolt for the door. Then I was racing off into the night, buck naked and grinning wide as I heard the scrabble of his paws on the hardwood behind me.

I let myself sink into the experience: my feet pounding over the dirt and leaves of the forest floor, the cool evening air and the lush garden of scents rushing in and out of my lungs, the thrill of the chase making my blood spark. My reflexes were lightning quick now, allowing me to be unnervingly silent as I tore through the trees and the bushes, leaping over ground obstacles and weaving among the thick trunks in order to throw him off my trail.

When I got to an especially large tree I lept at it, sinking my claws into the bark and hauling myself up to the lowest branch, the burn in my muscles and the scrape of bark against my skin flaming my arousal hotter. I would make it hard for Chris to catch me, but I had every faith that he would.

The beast in me demanded this ritual, snarling at me to run so he could catch, so we could fuck like animals in the dirt, under the moon.

I could hear him coming up on me, the predator to my prey. I hunched closer to the bough I was perched on, holding my breath and searching hard for a flicker of his form. Once I was sure he'd passed me I'd drop down and head back in the other direction, try and throw him off my trail.

But after a moment I couldn't hear anything, his scent still close but no other sign of him nearby. I tensed, my pulse pounding a frantic tempo in my ears. I grinned into the dark. He was truly hunting me now, stalking me from somewhere I couldn't even guess at. My sex was dripping with need, my skin so sensitized by tension and my sprint through the forest I was shivering.

He was on me before I could react, his big body slamming into me from a neighboring tree, big furry arms wrapping around me tight and spinning us in the air so that he took the brunt of the fall.

My Chris, ever the gentleman.

I tried to wriggle free, but it was more for show than anything; he'd caught me, and now I wanted him to take his prize.

He clamped his hands onto my hips, hauling me up his body from his position on his back with his new unnatural strength until I was sitting on his face, spread wide for him. He was on me with a snarl that sounded rabid, his hypermobile tongue slithering through my folds. I was so turned on that when he swirled that tongue of his over my clit it was almost too much. I was rocking my hips into his mouth, heedless of his sharp teeth because the intermittent prickles only wound me up tighter, and I healed quickly now anyway. When I came his tongue speared into my channel, one of his fingers replacing his tongue on my clit, driving my pleasure higher, making me unspool from my body with a piercing cry.

Then I was being spun, the world around me moving so fast I was losing track of where I was in it, until I found myself on my hands and knees on the forest floor. I felt his hands back on my hips, his hot breath on my back as he nipped at my shoulder, tongue lapping at the beautiful ring or silvery scar tissue from where he'd bit me to make me turn.

He slammed himself into me in one hard thrust up to his knot, driving the air from my lungs and making me see stars. He set a punishing pace, fingers digging into me hard enough to bruise, but I loved it, slamming my hips back into him, goading him on, begging him with my body, with my cries, to take me harder, faster, the creature in me calling for blood.

"Am I hurting you?" he asked me, pausing to check in. I laughed, shooting him a smile over my shoulder.

"Absolutely not," I growled, and then I was airborne again, still impaled on his thick cock, laid out on my back beneath him.

"Good," he grinned, needle-sharp teeth glinting in the moonlight, and then he was rutting into me like a man possessed, driving my body into the ground. He rose onto his knees, grabbing my legs and laying them over his elbows, spreading me wider for him. I started panting, tense and aching for what I knew was next, and then there it was, finally—the burning stretch of his knot breaching me, the pain barely there before it was obliterated by the pleasure of it rubbing incessantly over my g-spot, bringing another orgasm barreling through my body.

When I came back to my senses it was to Chris hovering above me, grinning like a demon, long tongue darting out to lick his lips. "You look so beautiful when you come for me, Anna," he groaned, letting my legs down so he could press in close again. "You think you've got one more in you?"

I nodded, brain too scrambled to speak, and I dipped one of my hands into the weeping mess of my pussy, my fingers working carefully at my swollen too-sensitive clit until the sensation shifted and I was winding back up again, pleasure strong enough to take my breath away and gray out my vision overtaking me. Chris murmured filthy encouragement in my ear, his tongue lapping at my neck, my ear, plunging into my mouth as I came again with a scream that startled a small animal out of the brush nearby, Chris following me over with two more brutal thrusts.

We lay there panting, locked together by the knot still swollen inside of me and trading tender kisses and sweet words completely at odds with the filthy things we'd just been doing. "I love you so much," he whispered, nuzzling at my face and breathing in my scent at my throat.

"And I love you," I promised back, wrapping my arms around his neck and holding him tight. "'Til death do us part."

* * *